Testim

I met Laura when she came to r.
that she was battling stage III breast cancer. As I got to know Laura
more, I found her to be a strong, hopeful, and resilient person. No
way was she going to let cancer get the best of her. What touched
me most was learning that she had two young children and how she
managed to teach them the true meaning of hope and strength. As a
mother of two wonderful daughters myself, I could not fathom how
I would even begin to break the news to my children. I knew that
it was tough for Laura at first to even think about how she would
tell her children—how can it not be? But I learned from Laura that
honesty and bravery were the ways to move forward to improve her
relationship with her children and improve her health. It's been ten
years since I first met Laura. She's fully recovered from her disease
and is stronger and healthier than ever! Congratulations to Laura
for inspiring others and sharing her experience.

Best wishes,
Erlene Chiang, DAOM, LAc

Laura Vidal is a talented author bringing her experience as a
breast cancer survivor and the wisdom of opening this challenging
conversation up to children. She provides a beautiful demystify-
ing explanation for children and adults to understand the positive
power of healing from breast cancer. The images and language
provide a poetry of wisdom embedded within the depth of heart
and compassion for those we love who engage in the healing process together. A treasure.

Dr. Ellen Hammerle
Ellen Hammerle, Ph.D., LMFT

Maggie

LIVES WITH

Breast Cancer

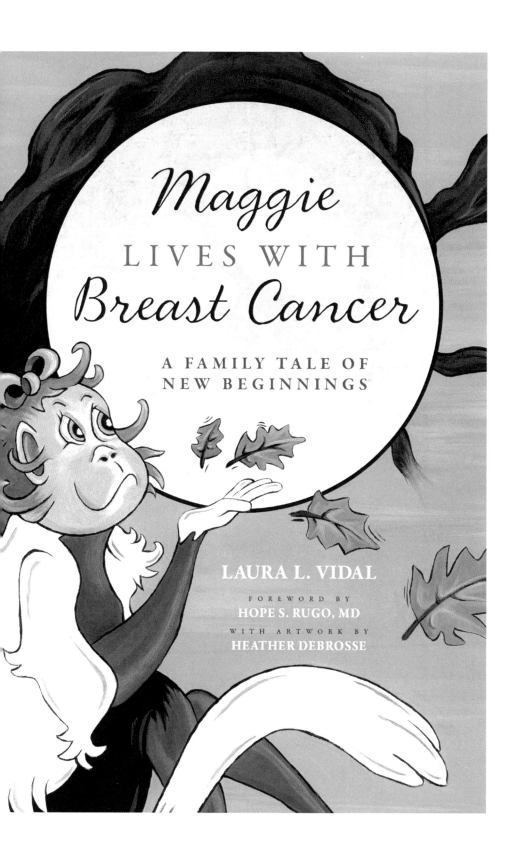

Maggie
LIVES WITH
Breast Cancer

A FAMILY TALE OF
NEW BEGINNINGS

LAURA L. VIDAL

FOREWORD BY
HOPE S. RUGO, MD

WITH ARTWORK BY
HEATHER DEBROSSE

Maggie Lives with Breast Cancer

Copyright © 2018 by Laura L. Vidal. All Rights Reserved.

For information about this title or to order other books and/or electronic media, contact the publisher:
lauralvidal.com

Library of Congress Control Number: 2016916156

ISBNs: 978-0-9974804-9-8 (hardcover)
         978-0-9974804-8-1 (softcover)
         978-0-9974804-2-9 (eBook)

Printed in the United States of America

Cover and Interior Design: 1106 Design
Book Cover Text: Graham Van Dixhorn, Write to Your Market, Inc.

Publisher's Cataloging-in-Publication
(Provided by Quality Books, Inc.)

Vidal, Laura L., author.
    Maggie lives with breast cancer : a family tale of
new beginnings / Laura L. Vidal ; foreword by Hope S.
Rugo ; illustrations by Heather Debrosse.
    pages cm
    SUMMARY: An inspiring story of one monkey's journey
through the acute treatments for breast cancer, and
includes Maggie's relationships with her husband, her
children and her community.
    Audience: Ages 0–12.
    LCCN 2016916156
    ISBN 978-0-9974804-9-8 (hardcover)
    ISBN 978-0-9974804-8-1 (paperback)
    ISBN 978-0-9974804-2-9 (eBook)

    1. Breast--Cancer--Juvenile fiction. 2. Breast--
Cancer--Diagnosis--Juvenile fiction. 3. Breast--Cancer
--Patients--Family relationships--Juvenile fiction.
4. Monkeys--Juvenile fiction. [1. Breast--Cancer--Fiction.
2. Breast--Cancer--Diagnosis--Fiction. 3. Breast--
Cancer--Patients--Family relationships--Fiction.
4. Monkeys--Fiction. 5. Cancer--Fiction.]   I. Debrosse,
Heather, illustrator. II. Title.

PZ7.1.V533Mag 2017   [Fic]
                QBI16-900047

I dedicate this book to my two beautiful, loving daughters, Ashley and Amber, who inspire me to continue on my spiritual healing path. Thank you both for visiting as many zoos as we could in the United States and internationally. We always looked for colobus monkeys first in the monkey area. My fond memories of our family visiting zoos inspired me to write the story of Maggie and her family.

Maggie Lives with Breast Cancer is an inspiring story of one monkey's journey through the acute treatments for breast cancer, and includes Maggie's relationships with her husband, her children and her community.

Drawing on her own personal experience, Laura Vidal paints a heartwarming picture full of hope and healing, along with embedded helpful suggestions about communication with children about serious parental illness. The illustrations are beautiful and help to create a book that will be treasured by children and parents alike.

— Hope S. Rugo, MD
Professor of Medicine
Director, Breast Oncology and Clinical Trials Education
University of California San Francisco
Helen Diller Family Comprehensive Cancer Center

Heather DeBrosse created wonderful illustrations.

"With a degree of fine arts from CCA (California College of the Arts), majoring in Illustration/Graphic Design, I've always had a passion for character design/children's book illustrations. I was honored that Laura Vidal contacted me to illustrate such a meaningful children's book that had such a personal connection to her.

The process we shared through creating Maggie Lives with Breast Cancer *has been satisfying and fulfilling, and I am thrilled to see Laura's vision come to life through this amazing story. I look forward to future adventures from 'Maggie' and life-learning experiences!"*

— Heather DeBrosse

Thank you to my mom and dad, additional family members, friends, and community, whose continued support helped me thrive. A special thanks to all the health care providers who are committed to helping me survive: Dr. H. Rugo, Dr. B. McDougall, Dr. E. Chiang, Dr. B. Fowble, Dr. S. Hwang, Dr. M. Goldman, Dr. L. Way, Dr. J. Chan, Dr. R. Foster, Dr. G. Kind, Grace Janho, Dr. Ellen Hammerle, Stacey DeGooyer, Dr. K. Bixby, Dr. Francesca McCartney, Michael McCartney and Angie Chen. A special thanks to Vivienne E. Miller. I am grateful to Rick Ramirez, who has cut my hair for more than eighteen years. Rick knew me well enough to suggest that I wear hats.

*M*aggie and Mark held hands in silence. Each lost in their own thoughts as they gazed at the moon during the shortest night this year. Glad their children were asleep. They now had a chance to discuss Sam the Veterinarian's conclusion of testing Maggie's lump and suggestion of Sam's plan. Mark commented to Maggie how proud he was of her for caring enough about her body to notice changes. Maggie felt comforted. She was grateful for Mark's company. Both were relieved the wait for answers was over. "Tonight we will reflect on ways to help our family heal and grow closer," said Mark. Maggie agreed. Maggie and Mark realized they needed to shift some of their attitudes and beliefs. Both were concerned about helping their children understand what Maggie may experience as she heals. An agreement was made to discuss with their children right away over breakfast. Half-asleep, they anxiously awaited dawn.

Summer began today, the longest day of the year, which is also known as the summer solstice.

Mark held Maggie's hand while they ate breakfast with their children—Madeline, age eight, and Max, age four. Maggie was having a hard time swallowing her food. She knew what she was about to share with her children would change their lives forever.

"Mom, are you okay?" asked Madeline. "You seem different today."

"You're right, my beautiful daughter. Things are different for me today. We have some news to share with both of you before we tell other family and friends," said Maggie. "I went to our vet yesterday, and he gave me some bad news. The test is called a biopsy and it revealed my lump is cancerous. Now, it's bad news because I'm sick, but the good news is that I can get treatment. With the kind of breast cancer I have, first I'll have chemotherapy, then surgery to remove the lump, and finish up with radiation treatments to make sure no bad cells are sneaking around. The goal is to stop any more breast cancer cells from growing in my body.

"I understand this is a lot of information, and I will explain each treatment. All of this feels a bit overwhelming, but let's try to rest and enjoy our summer. We will gain emotional and physical strength to support each other."

The family circled together, hugging one another for an extremely long time before another word was spoken.

After the long embrace, all four had tears streaming down their faces. Madeline and Max said in unison, "Mom, did we make you get the disease?"

Relieved to hear Madeline and Max express their concern, Mark hugged the children while Maggie explained.

"Don't you dare blame yourselves! Children are not responsible for a parent contracting breast cancer or any other disease. Your body's ability to eliminate

toxins can affect your health. Sometimes our bodies become sick from the foods we eat or don't eat—like your vegetables—or from toxicity, or even from the land and air around us."

Madeline and Max knew their mom was right. They weren't to blame.

Max said, "Mom, I know you can beat this!"

Madeline sniffled and agreed. "Dad, can I catch breast cancer from Mom?" she asked.

"Good question, dear. No, you cannot." Mark assured all of them that, as a family, they would support Maggie. Together they would tell the rest of their family members, friends, and their community.

Putting one paw in front of the other, Maggie began her journey toward recovery.

Madeline and Max began their nighttime rituals before going to sleep. Dad asked Madeline to read an inspirational story to her brother about a family experiencing breast cancer from a new book Maggie had recently bought. Madeline grumbled to herself while climbing into bed.

I can't believe I am going to read this book to my little brother before we go to sleep, thought Madeline. She looked over at his sad eyes and put her arm around

him. Madeline took a deep breath and began reading while Max drew a picture.

"I can't believe Mom is sick," said Madeline. Max was scared about what might happen to his mom. He was glad his sister read the story. Max asked Madeline if he could tell his best friend about his mom having cancer. Madeline smiled and said, "That is a good idea. I will also let my best friend know tomorrow."

Madeline realized her parents were right about reading the story with Max. "Sweet dreams, Max," said his sister.

"We are blessed to have such wonderful children," said Mark. Maggie agreed.

Both were in tears when the story was over. Once they heard their children sleeping, they went in and kissed them goodnight. A storm picked up and raged all night, and they continued to hold hands in the darkness. Mark's mood was as dark as the clouds outside, as he fretted over his beautiful, loving wife. He held Maggie close, protecting her from the squall and what their future may bring. They dozed off with dried tears on their faces.

It was dawn on the last day of summer. Maggie and Mark rose early hugging one another as they watched the sun begin to rise. Mark said to Maggie, "We did manage to enjoy the summer together honey.

We have overcome obstacles as a family, and we will continue to do so." Maggie agreed. Then she burst into laughter and reminded Mark about how the kids would sometimes sneak up and surprise them. "I never get tired of them doing it," said Maggie.

Mark smiled and agreed that playing jokes on each other was fun this summer.

"Let's let Max and Madeline's dreams stay sweet just a little longer before we wake them for our special family day. Today I just want to feel normal," said Maggie.

Maggie's treatment began the day of the fall equinox, when night and day were of equal length, reminding Maggie to lead a more balanced life. For Maggie, it was the perfect time to begin treatment.

Maggie was scared but relieved. Mark comforted her as they traversed the trees to Sam's Vet Hospital. Her friends were taking care of Madeline and Max and had promised a home-cooked meal upon their return.

Grateful, she focused on healing thoughts while Mark held her hand during the several hours it took for her first treatment of chemotherapy, or the use of chemicals to control breast cancer. She felt her anxiety and stress lessening with every tick of the clock.

"Will you look at Mom! Dad said she would start losing her fur after the first chemotherapy treatment, and he was right," said Madeline.

"Mom, you've had some bad fur days in the past," said Max, batting at the large tuft of his mother's coat that sat on the floor, "but we can't imagine Mom having *no* fur days!"

"Mom, your shedding is scary!" said Madeline.

"Honey, it's normal to feel scared and confused," said Maggie. "Children, look at the beauty of the trees as they lose their leaves." Maggie pointed to

the leaves as a breeze blew several brightly colored fronds past. "My fur will continue to fall out just like those leaves."

Maggie had thought about shaving the remaining fur on her head but realized it was too much for her to handle on her own. When she had asked Mark for help, he had also been uncomfortable with the idea, so Maggie decided it was time to see her fur stylist.

When Maggie visited Rick, her fur stylist, he was prepared for her. He shaved the fur off her head and gave her a beautiful pink bandana as a gift.

Maggie was ecstatic.

"Rick, you have lifted my spirits! The veterinarian recommended eight rounds of treatment. A month after the last round is finished, my fur will begin to grow back. I know some monkeys prefer fur pieces, but I like the idea of an attractive bandana. My head will be warm and stylish. I already feel better about myself."

"There are so many beautiful, different-colored bandanas to wear! I am so grateful you picked out my first one and for one less decision I have to make. I feel overwhelmed by the number of things I have to decide every day. Today you made my life easier by thinking about how I could look my best. I trust your decision. Wow, I feel great right now."

Although Maggie's head was shaved so that no more fur would fall out like the leaves, she was in pain, and her exhaustion increased. She took time to reflect on her experience while undergoing chemotherapy and was relieved that her last round of treatment would be right before Thanksgiving.

Family and friends prepared a holiday dinner for everyone, and Maggie was thankful for many things, including her pink bandana. Without her furry coat covering her from head to toe, she wore the bandana around the clock to help her stay warm.

She cried tears of joy and sadness as she braced herself for surgery after Thanksgiving.

As their immediate and extended family gathered to enjoy the Thanksgiving feast, Maggie asked each monkey to share what he or she was grateful for that day. She added that she was grateful for enjoying a delicious meal and for feeling well.

Mark was grateful to have everyone together. Madeline was pleased she had gotten her mother to laugh and realized she and Max could still have fun with their mom.

Max and Madeline were happy because before they sat down to eat, their mom had gotten to play with them, which she hadn't had the strength for in a long time. When they played with her, they had been very careful to keep her from getting too tired.

The joy Maggie felt when playing with her children gave her the courage to embrace the next procedure.

Mark and Maggie walked toward Sam's Vet Hospital in silence on the morning of her surgery. The surgeon's task was to remove the lump from Maggie's breast.

Maggie kept thinking positive thoughts for the best possible outcome. Feeling comforted by their silence, Mark opened the door for Maggie and kept his thoughts to himself as Sam prepared Maggie for surgery. Mark held her hand.

Sam saw concern on Mark's face and reassured him that he had experience with this surgery, and he anticipated no complications.

The children nervously waited at home with extended family, anxious to know if the surgery went well.

The veterinarian's predictions had been right. Maggie's surgery went well.

Maggie stayed at Sam's for a few days until she was strong enough to go home. Her family was thrilled to have her back. Her entire community came together and provided at least one meal a day for her family.

Maggie really appreciated the support she received and tried to express just how much each of the monkeys meant to her.

Her family, friends, and community assured her they were more than happy that they could help.

Grateful that Maggie was doing well with her treatment, her mom decided to gather her entire community to celebrate.

During the event, Maggie took a deep breath and told her friends it was time to do the three Rs:

Rest—Maggie's body needed proper sleep to heal.

Recover—Maggie sought outside support with a group called the Sunflowers. The Sunflowers were breast cancer–surviving monkeys in various stages of recovery who met with a health care professional from time to time to answer any questions they may have.

Rejoice—Maggie was happy she had completed chemotherapy and that her surgery was also behind her. She was tired and sore, but her mood was one of contentment. Maggie felt love and support from family, friends, and the community. Now she was inspired to prepare herself for the last phase of treatment.

The winter solstice was the longest night of the year, and Maggie allowed her body to enjoy the extra

rest the night provided as she began radiation treatments. Radiation therapy uses beams of intense energy to kill cancer cells.

The veterinarian had determined the number of treatments each monkey would receive. In Maggie's case, the recommendation had been twenty-five treatments.

She traversed the trees herself to Sam's for treatment, taking her time to ponder the meaning of the winter solstice. Maggie's body felt exactly like one of the trees whose leaves had fallen off. Looking at the barren winter branches, she began to value the importance of nutrition.

Each day after leaving radiation, Maggie thought of something she was grateful for in that moment. Once she got home, she ate something nutritious.

Implementing the three Rs was helping her heal, but Maggie was depleted from all her treatments. Now that she had a plan, it was time to get Mark, Madeline, and Max to improve their eating habits as well so that they could all lead healthier lives.

Maggie forgave herself for not paying enough attention to nutrition before. She asked the Sunflowers' health care professional and other monkeys for all the tips, suggestions, and ideas they had.

The first thing was to drink more water, and the nutritionist suggested eating a variety of fruits, vegetables, healthy fats, and protein.

Following the Sunflowers' nutritional guidelines, Mark prepared a healthy meal for the family to eat together.

"Dad, I know Mom needs to eat healthier, but why do we?" asked Max.

"It is important for all of us to care about what we put in our bodies. Your mom feels our support when we cooperate and eat what she is eating," said Mark.

"Okay, I will do my best to care more about what I put in my body," said Madeline.

Reluctant, Max also agreed. Maggie happily enjoyed her meal.

Groundhog Day was February 2, and everyone waited as the groundhog predicted an early spring.

Maggie and Mark celebrated by removing Maggie's bandana. Soft, fuzzy fur was covering her head.

Maggie was elated as the darkness of her treatments and experience with the disease faded. An inner peace and wisdom helped Maggie face the transformations that were soon to come.

On the spring equinox, Maggie contemplated the importance of the three Rs. Resting, recovering, rejoicing, and following a good nutrition plan had helped her lead a healthier life.

In ancient times, the spring equinox was known as "the day on which the earth began." The day represented rebirth and also transformation. The spring

equinox, like the fall equinox, is one of the two days of the year when night and day were of equal length. To Maggie, that represented balance, and she realized how important it was for her to lead not only a healthier life, but also a more balanced life. As she enjoyed the spring equinox, she reflected on the progress she had made toward that goal.

With her treatments now complete, Maggie rejoiced!
She was grateful she had implemented the three Rs.
Spring was her new beginning.

Maggie was relieved that the most difficult part of recovery was behind her. She was fatigued and still didn't always feel well, but she gave herself permission to take time, energy, and space to heal. Maggie realized how blessed she was. Other monkeys hadn't recovered as well as she had.

On one beautiful spring morning, Maggie, her friends, and her family slid on their sunglasses and enjoyed the health and prosperity life had given them. They shared a few laughs over a meal, and one thing became very clear to Maggie: Surrounded by family, friends, and community, she could overcome any obstacle in her path.

Thank you to following friends, neighbors and family for supporting this project: Len Poncia, CJ and Chris Finley, Matthew Turton, Catherine Way, Guthrie Morgan, Tricia Barrett, Ron, Amy Schoew, Lynn Anderson Poole, Marsha & Tom Dugan, Davy Crockett & Mara Meisner, Mike & Tracie Waxman, Sadie Waxman, May Ng Lee, Martha Angove, Rose Barlow, Whitney & Phil Arnautou, Robina Riccitiello and Joo-Hee Bae.

Made in the USA
Middletown, DE
31 August 2019